THE JUNIOR NOVELIZATION

ISBN 978-0-7364-3230-6

randomhouse.com/kids

Printed in the United States of America

10 9 8 7 6 5 4 3 2 1

THE JUNIOR NOVELIZATION

Adapted by Suzanne Francis

Random House 🏠 New York

ZIP-ZIP-ZIP! Eight planes zoomed around a course, racing over the barren desert. The grandstands were filled with thousands of cheering cars, planes, and trucks, all watching the race with great anticipation.

The roar of the fans really got Dusty Crophopper's engine going. It was a sharp contrast to what he used to hear back in his days working as a crop duster. Flying over the cornfields in the early hours of the morning was a quiet, lonely job. The occasional rustling of the wind through the cornstalks and the quiet hum of his sprayer were the only sounds for miles. The crowd was far more exciting to listen to! Dusty was also thrilled by the revving of his engine as he pushed himself to get ahead. He truly loved to race.

Dusty trailed behind a few other planes . . . but not for long. He pushed hard as the needle on his torque gauge climbed. Dusty knew he would have to use maximum power to win the race, and he wasn't afraid to do it. He tore around the posts, weaving his way to the head of the pack. He could see the finish line in the distance as he inched up behind the leading racer. His engine buzzed as he strained and pushed even harder.

Brent Mustangberger, the best sportscaster on the Racing Sports Network, leaned forward to speak through the PA. "Look at them go! Into the final lap!"

VROOOOOM!

"And here comes number seven—Dusty Crophopper!" Brent's words rang out across the desert as the crowd went wild. Dusty's best friends from Propwash Junction— Chug, Dottie, Skipper, and Sparky—were in the crowd. They hooted and hollered with all their might as Dusty crossed the finish line first.

It was true that Dusty loved racing for its own sake, but nothing compared to the rush of winning. He was more than happy to scribble autographs for adoring fans and smile for pictures after the race.

Dusty had been on tour for a while and was winning again and again, collecting trophies, giving television interviews, and appearing in magazines and newspapers. He had become a very famous airplane.

Back in Propwash Junction, everyone crowded around a tiny television to watch Dusty's interview with Brent Mustangberger.

"Dusty, you were just a small-town crop duster who overcame impossible odds to win the Wings Around The Globe Rally and become an air-racing legend!"

"Well, Brent," said Dusty, "I've had an amazing team supporting me every step of the way. The best coach, the best mechanic, and the best fuel truck anyone could ask for!" Dusty was calm and cool on television, and it was just like him to be modest and thank his friends in Propwash. Skipper, Dottie, Chug, and Sparky couldn't help smiling when he mentioned them.

"I'd say you've come a long way since those crop-dusting days!" added Brent.

"Racing is all I ever wanted to do—it's my life!" Dusty said sincerely.

When Dusty returned home to Propwash Junction, everyone at the Fill 'n' Fly, the garage and fueling station, was enjoying all the magazine and newspaper articles about Dusty.

"Awesome pic, Dust! 'Cept your eyes are closed." Sparky smiled as he looked proudly at the picture of his friend in the newspaper. He carried the paper over to Dusty, who was getting some oil from his buddy Chug, the fuel truck.

"Racing with your eyes closed," said Chug with a smile. "So that's your secret!"

Mayday, an old fire truck who wore thick black-rimmed eyeglasses, rolled up. "That was some pretty fancy flyin', Dusty!" he said. Mayday told Dusty he'd watched the race on his "radio with pictures."

As much as Dusty loved racing, he was always happy to get back to his friends. Propwash Junction was just a tiny little farm town in the middle of the country, but it was home to everyone Dusty loved most.

"Guys, listen to this!" Sparky read from the newspaper. "'After his Red Bulldozer win, Dusty Crophopper—'"

"That's you," Chug interrupted, nodding to Dusty.

"'—returns home to Propwash Junction—'"

"That's here," Mayday added.

"'—where he will be performing at their annual Corn Festival.'" Sparky looked up from behind the newspaper proudly.

The Corn Festival was a Propwash tradition, and everyone in town looked forward to it all year long. The festival was full of corn-themed food, entertainment, contests, costumes, and music, and plenty of corny fun. The gang couldn't believe it—the Corn Festival was national news! With that kind of press, this year's festival would be ginormous!

"This is going to put Propwash Junction on the map!" Chug added.

"Ooh, I've always wanted to be on a map," said Sparky.

Everyone in town could hardly contain their excitement. The motel's phone was already ringing off the hook, and the owners said they'd have to get out the inflatable hangars to accommodate all the visitors! Dusty was happy to see everyone in Propwash coming together for the festival. He knew it was going to be the biggest and best one yet!

"Dusty!" Skipper called. Skipper had taught Dusty how to race and had prepared him for the Wings Around The Globe Rally. Besides being Dusty's coach and very good friend, Skipper was also a World War II veteran who had flown with the Jolly Wrenches squadron in the navy. "Ready to do some flyin'?" he asked the world-famous racer.

"Absolutely, Skipper," Dusty replied.

The sun was making its way into the clear blue sky,

beginning to light up a perfectly beautiful day. Dusty rolled onto the taxiway, and Skipper followed.

They revved their engines, turned toward the end of the runway, and prepared for takeoff. As much as Dusty loved racing and traveling to far-off places, it always felt good to be home, flying with Skipper. "Hey, Propwash Tower, this is Crophopper Seven. Flight of two ready for takeoff."

"Crophopper Seven, Propwash Tower. Wind calm, runway two-seven cleared for takeoff. Have a great flight, fellas."

Their engines roared as they cruised down the runway and rose into the air. They retracted their landing gear and soared gracefully across the sky, passing the water tower, proudly painted with the words PROPWASH JUNCTION—HOME OF RACING CHAMPION DUSTY CROPHOPPER.

Dusty and Skipper made a wide arc through the crisp air, feeling the warmth of the morning sun on their wings. After a moment, Dusty broke off, zigzagging this way and that around grain elevators while Skipper flew along, watching him closely.

"Snap into those turns!" Skipper yelled. "Tighten it up."

Dusty took Skipper's advice and adjusted his wings. "There ya go!"

Dusty flew between the trees, then glided over the river. With Skipper behind him, he followed the river's winding path, skimming the surface of the sparkling water.

"Now let's work the vertical!" Skipper said.

Dusty grinned as he revved his engine, gearing up for the vertical climb. He had to gain a lot of speed to pull it off. He dove beneath an old railroad bridge and then pushed his engine as he climbed straight up, higher and higher until . . . *PTT! PTT! PTTTTT!* Suddenly, his engine stuttered.

Dusty paused and tried to figure out what was going on. *PTT! PTT! PTTTTT!* His engine stuttered again. *Uh-oh,* Dusty thought. Something was definitely not right. He shuddered as his insides rattled and whirled. He didn't feel well at all. Before he could think of what to do, he began to spin out of control.

Skipper pulled up next to him. "Dusty? Dusty? What's wrong?"

"My engine . . ." Dusty was out of breath and unable to finish his sentence. He was losing altitude fast and felt weak. The sound of the wind rushing by as he spiraled toward the ground was sickening.

Skipper had to get Dusty safely to the ground as quickly as possible. "Propwash Tower, this is Jolly Wrench Seven—we're a flight of two, five miles north of the airport, inbound for a precautionary landing."

As they approached the runway, Skipper guided Dusty in and the two landed safely. They headed straight for Dottie's Garage. Dottie, a forklift and Dusty's good friend and trusted mechanic, would be able to figure out what had gone wrong out there. Sparky gave Dusty an oil change as Skipper waited nearby.

"I don't know what it was. I wasn't doing anything different," Dusty said as Dottie carefully investigated his panel. "You know, pylon turns, a vertical . . . like we do every day. I mean, I feel great."

Dottie sighed and headed over to her worktable. She sprayed water on an air filter to remove large metallic chunks from it. They landed in a petri dish. "I've got a love/hate relationship with you, Dusty," she said. "Love that you're my best customer; hate what you're doing to yourself."

As usual, Dusty thought Dottie was overreacting. He knew she was protective of him, but he felt fine—how could anything be wrong?

Dottie placed the metallic chunks beneath a microscope, and an enlarged view of the metal appeared on a nearby monitor. She dropped liquid acid onto them and red smoke appeared. Dottie sighed. She clearly was not happy with the results, but Dusty didn't notice. He was too busy thinking about his next big race.

"And, hey, the Speed City Airfest is just a few weeks away. And I think if I get a little more speed coming out of my turns, really work that radial G, I can definitely improve my time. Yeah, I'm feelin' good about my next race."

Dottie faced Dusty. "Well, no damage to the casing or compressor blades."

"See, I told you. Just a hiccup, that's all," Dusty said, ready to move on.

"But there is—" Before Dottie could continue, Chug barreled into the garage.

"Dusty! Dusty! What happened? Are you okay, Dust?" Chug was worried about his friend, but Dusty quickly assured him that he was fine. He told Chug that Dottie had checked him out and found nothing.

Frustrated, Dottie took a deep breath and blurted out the news: "Your reduction gearbox is failing."

The room fell quiet.

"My . . . my gearbox?"

"Your chip detector had a cluster of steel shavings on it. Flakes from the gears. That's what caused the trouble."

Dusty didn't understand why Dottie seemed so gloomy. Couldn't she just order another gearbox and replace it? She would be able to fix him right up.

Dottie gazed at Dusty.

"What?" Dusty pressed her for an answer.

"Your gearbox, it's . . . it's out of production," Dottie said. She couldn't even remember the last time she had seen one. It had been discontinued a long time ago.

"But, Dottie, c'mon, can't you just build Dust a new one?" Chug asked hopefully.

"No, it's too complex. It has to be factory," Dottie answered.

Dusty couldn't believe what he was hearing. How could he be unfixable?

"From now on, you have to back off the torque," Dottie told him. "Keep it under eighty percent."

"What? Eighty percent? Dottie, you've got me cranked to one-forty! I need that to race!"

Dottie stared at Dusty sternly. "If you push yourself into the red, your gearbox will fail."

Dusty didn't want to hear this. "But—no, no, no, Dottie—"

"And then the engine will seize—"

Dusty wondered if maybe the test was wrong. He had a race coming up. He couldn't deal with this.

"You'll crash." Dottie repeated it, to make sure Dusty was listening: "You push yourself into the red, you crash."

Dottie installed a warning light on Dusty's panel.

"If the light comes on, you'll need to pull power—slow down."

"But, Dottie . . . you're saying . . . I can't race anymore." Dusty was heartbroken.

"I am so sorry."

Chug, Sparky, and Skipper were at a loss for words, and a grim silence hung over the garage.

Later that night, the neon sign in front of Honkers Sports Bar buzzed and flickered to life as darkness fell over Propwash Junction. A typical crowd packed the room. Honky-tonk music played, and cars and trucks danced, talked, and laughed. Everyone was drinking cans of oil and having a great time . . . except Dusty.

Then Chug and Sparky showed up, full of excitement. They had just gotten off the radio with someone they knew in Grand Flaps.

"He's got the gearbox?" Dusty asked impatiently.

Chug and Sparky explained that their friend didn't have the gearbox, but he did know someone with twenty-one service hangars. That guy said he'd check his inventory and put the word out to try to find Dusty a gearbox.

"It's a great start!" said Sparky enthusiastically.

"'Cause if that gearbox is out there, we'll find it for ya, buddy," Chug added.

Dusty smiled. Even though he felt broken, it sure was nice to have such great friends.

Just then, Leadbottom rolled up. Leadbottom was an old biplane and had been Dusty's boss when Dusty worked as a crop duster. "And, hey, if ya don't, it's all right. Because the answer is YES!"

Dusty looked at Leadbottom, confused.

"Yes, of course you can have your old job back! Don't even have to bother askin'. That's the kinda guy I am," the senior crop duster said proudly.

"Leadbottom," Skipper said, rolling forward, trying to make him stop talking. But there seemed to be no stopping Leadbottom.

"Course, I'll have to start you back at minimum

wage, and you've lost all your vacation time and other various benefits, but . . . ," Leadbottom continued.

"Leadbottom, please; I'm sure Dusty appreciates your offer, but now's not the best—"

Leadbottom was not picking up on Skipper's hints. "C'mon, Skipper. I could get his old sprayer back from that Germany place, have it cleaned up and bolted back on him in no time." Leadbottom made obnoxiously loud drilling noises as he pretended to bolt Dusty's old sprayer back on.

Finally, Skipper offered to buy Leadbottom a can of oil just to get rid of him.

"I'm tellin' ya, Skip, it's the truth. Other than me, Dusty is the best duster I've ever known."

"And I'm telling you that Dusty don't crop dust no more," Chug said angrily.

"That's right. No more!" Sparky chimed in.

"He's a racer," said Chug.

"A racer!"

"And he's gonna be back to racing in no time," added Chug.

"In no time!"

"Right, Dusty?"

"Right, Dust?"

Chug and Sparky looked over, but Dusty was gone. They hadn't noticed, but while Leadbottom was going on and on about Dusty working as a crop duster again, Dusty had snuck out of the bar.

Dusty wanted to be alone. He couldn't even think about going back to dusting crops. Alone and sad, he went for a solo night flight, soaring high over Propwash Junction. He just couldn't believe what was happening. How was it that just a few short hours ago, he had been flying with Skipper and everything was okay? Things had been going so well for him. Now his whole world had shifted. How had it fallen apart so quickly?

Dusty stared at his torque gauge as he flew faster and faster. He was angry. He was a racer, and racers needed speed. They needed to push their engines to race. And if Dusty couldn't race, what would he do? It was all he'd ever wanted to do with his life.

With his eyes fixed on his gauge, Dusty ascended higher into the air, picking up speed. He watched as the needle climbed toward the yellow zone. He continued, flying faster and faster, pushing his engine so hard that the ground beneath him began to blur. Dusty locked his eyes on the torque gauge, mesmerized, as the needle crept closer and closer to where the yellow met the red. The needle was about a hair's breadth from the red line when . . . *FLASH! FLASH! FLASH!* The red warning light came on.

Dusty slowed down to bring the needle back to the yellow zone, and the light stopped flashing. But then he noticed another flashing red light. It wasn't his warning light. Where was it coming from? Dusty looked up and saw that the wire suspension tower was flashing its light—and it was right in front of him! He tried to dodge it, but his wing clipped the top of the tower!

Ahhhhhh!

The tower light popped, and sparks rained down like fireworks against the night sky.

Dusty was unable to gain control. He breathed heavily as he spiraled toward the ground. He tried to adjust himself, but he continued to plummet toward the earth until . . . *CRASH!*

He landed too far down the runway, and he was going fast! He careened onto the taxiway but couldn't stop. He was headed straight toward the Fill 'n' Fly.

Dusty swerved this way and that but couldn't slow down. Finally, he slammed right into one of the station's support beams and rolled back slowly, coming to a stop. Phew! He was safe.

Seconds later, he heard a sickening creak coming from the support beam .... *CRASH!* The beam collapsed. Then the gas station's overhang dropped onto a gas pump. *KA-BOOM!* The pump exploded and a fire erupted! Dusty watched helplessly as the Fill 'n' Fly lit up like the Fourth of July, engulfed in flames.

"FIRE! FIRE!" Dusty yelled as loudly as he could.

Outside Honkers, Skipper, Sparky, and Chug stood wide-eyed as they took in the terrible sight of the Fill 'n' Fly being swallowed up by towering flames. They immediately sprang into action.

"I'll get Mayday!" Sparky said.

"I'll hit the shutoff valve!" Chug said, and the three sped off.

Sparky hurried into Mayday's fire station and pressed the emergency button. The rusty old fire bell let out a wimpy little ring and then rattled as the center bolt came loose and hit the floor with a *CLANK*. Mayday's fire station was definitely out of date. No one in Propwash could even remember the last time that bell had rung!

"Whoa!" said Mayday when he spotted the smoke. "I'm on it!" He sped off but quickly returned. "Had to get my glasses," he said with a chuckle, before racing off and knocking down the rickety firehouse sign on his way out.

Once on the scene, Mayday threw open his gate. Dottie and Sparky unrolled his fire hose and clasped it onto a hydrant. Then they threw a lever and watched the hose puff up as it filled with water. Mayday aimed his nozzle at the flames, but the old hose had lots of leaks! Sparky tried to cover each little hole, but the pressure built up and shot him straight across to Chug.

"I got ya," Chug said, catching Sparky.

With water spouting out of the holes, Mayday wound up with nothing more than a sad little dribble at the end of the hose. When he looked into the mouth of the hose—*DRIP!*—a lone drop leaked out, hitting him right between the eyes. The hose was *not* going to put out this fire. Mayday had to come up with a new plan fast. He fixed his eyes on the water tower, then looked at his friends behind him. "I'm gonna need some help," he said.

In no time at all, everyone was in position at the water tower. Dottie loosened one bolt from the tower's base, and Sparky pried up another. They wrapped the old fire hose around the legs of the tower, and everyone grabbed hold. Mayday hooked his winch cable to the tower and yelled, "Pull!"

Mayday, Skipper, Chug, and Dusty grunted as they pulled with all their might. The tower let out a long, low groan as it began to lean. The old hose frayed as the crew pulled harder and harder.

Suddenly, the tower tilted and collapsed, crashing onto its side. Water gushed in every direction, flooding the entire area and extinguishing the flames. The fire was finally out.

Dusty looked down to see one of the Corn Festival flyers floating among the burned pieces of metal and ash. He felt awful.

The next morning, a couple of representatives from the Transportation Management Safety Team (TMST) showed up to investigate the fire. The charred Fill 'n' Fly was quickly surrounded with bright yellow caution tape. Ryker, a strict aircraft rescue fire vehicle with a very serious expression, arrived with an uptight-looking forklift. They eyed Mayday as the gang stood by, concerned.

"TMS . . . T?" Chug asked.

"This Means Serious Trouble," said Sparky.

Dottie sighed. "Transportation Management Safety Team," she explained.

The TMST vehicles scattered orange safety cones around the area and then approached Mayday to discuss the fire. The forklift even put safety cones around poor Mayday! Then he harshly clicked his pen and began writing furiously in his notepad.

Ryker asked an uneasy Mayday a bunch of questions while the forklift took notes.

"Is, uh, is that guy writing down everything I say?" Mayday asked nervously.

"Yes," said Ryker.

"Well I—I . . . So he just wrote that down?" asked Mayday.

"Yes."

"And that?"

"Yes."

"And that?"

"Yessssss," said Ryker, getting frustrated. "Can you provide me with your self-inspection records and emergency procedure plans?"

Mayday chuckled timidly and explained that

Propwash Junction didn't have many emergencies. Ryker did not like that answer. Or when Mayday added, "Besides, we did get the fire out."

"Is that your contingency plan, Mr. Mayday?" Ryker asked in his monotone voice. "Every time there's an incident, you topple a water tower?" He was clearly not giving an inch.

Mayday was ashamed. He stood there, speechless.

Dusty stepped in. "This was my fault," he said. "I clipped a tower. I flew out last night 'cause I . . ." His voice sadly trailed off.

Mayday looked at his friend with understanding and whispered, "Dusty, it was an accident."

But Ryker did not want to hear any more. "It's clear that this airport has no plans for an emergency, and it has equipment from last century. So unless Mr. Mayday gets refurbished and acquires a second firefighting vehicle, in accordance with CFR title fourteen, volume three, chapter one, section one hundred thirty-nine, subparagraph B, I am pulling this airport's certificate of operation for noncompliance of rescue and firefighting regulations."

The forklift clicked his pen closed and tucked away

his notepad. Then he and Ryker took off, leaving everyone in shock. No one could believe it. Shutting down the airport meant shutting down the whole town! Without an active runway, no one could land.

Everyone in Propwash gathered around the main terminal to discuss the terrible news. They immediately started worrying about the Corn Festival. Would there even *be* a Corn Festival this year? If the town was closed, they'd have to cancel it. This was a disaster!

Skipper tried to get everyone to calm down. He and Dottie had a plan.

"This is Mayday now," said Dottie as Sparky held up a drawing of Mayday.

"I did the drawings," Chug said proudly.

"We add a new four-hundred-watt siren, a two-thousand-GPM roof turret, a high-capacity water tank with integrated class-A foam cell . . ."

Sparky dramatically switched the picture for a new one of Mayday that showed what he would look like after the upgrade. Mayday looked futuristic and totally cool!

"And we'll have an all-new Mayday!" Dottie said. The crowd started to feel better. Maybe they could save Propwash after all.

"Get out! He gets rocket boosters?" Sparky admired the picture with awe.

"Fueled by good 'ol hydrazine and nitrogen tetroxide! Course, that stuff's highly explosive, so you'll wanna keep it away from any open flames . . . ," Chug said.

"But he's a fire truck," said Sparky.

"Duh! Go on, Dottie," Chug said, trying to cover his error.

Dottie explained that once Mayday was updated, all they would need to reopen Propwash was a second firefighter. Again, panic set in among the crowd. Propwash didn't have the money to pay for a firefighter, and on top of that, it was fire season. They wouldn't even be able to find a volunteer at this point. It seemed like a hopeless situation.

Mayday sadly rolled toward his fire station. With the sun setting on the horizon, he adjusted his crooked fire station sign before he went inside.

Dusty quietly approached Mayday, who was sitting alone, staring at the back wall of his station.

"Uh . . . knock, knock," Dusty said softly, entering the station.

"Oh . . . hey, Dusty." Mayday looked at Dusty but

then turned back and continued to stare at the wall.

Dusty felt terrible. This whole mess was his fault. "I just, uh . . . I wish there was something I could do."

"Oh, there's nothing. It's all right. I'm . . ." Mayday's voice cracked. "I'm old, Dusty. Looks like my firefighting days are over."

Dusty looked at all of Mayday's memorabilia hanging on the wall. There were plaques, medals, pictures, and articles from his many years as a firefighter.

"No, no, Mayday, there's still plenty of firefight left in you," Dusty said, trying to boost his friend's spirits. He leaned in for a closer look at one of the plaques. "Look. I mean, right here: Firefighter of the Year."

"Nineteen sixty-eight," Mayday said dismissively.

"Okay. Your Bronze Star, " Dusty said, gesturing to the award.

"Old and tarnished . . . like me," Mayday said with a sigh.

Dusty came up to a picture he had never noticed before. He gazed at it closely, inspecting the scene. It looked like an old crop-dusting plane dropping water. "Umm . . . is this you and . . . and an old crop duster?" Dusty asked.

Finally, Mayday turned around and rolled over to Dusty. He squinted at the picture and explained that it showed one of the first aerial firefighters, a Single-Engine Air Tanker, also called a SEAT. "See, instead of dustin' crops—y'know, like you used to do—they dropped water."

"Wow." Suddenly, Dusty had an idea. "Mayday, what if . . . I became our second firefighter?"

"You? But—"

"Dottie'll fix you up. And I'll get certified," Dusty said, smiling.

"What about your racing?" Mayday asked.

"Look, right now, we need to get Propwash reopened . . . me and you," Dusty said confidently.

Mayday smiled at his friend, nearly in tears. "I don't know what to say. Thanks, Dusty."

Dusty knew it was the right thing to do, and for the first time since he'd found out about his gearbox, he felt hopeful about the future.

The next morning, Dusty was ready to go. He was going to fly to Piston Peak Air Attack Base and meet up with Mayday's old friend Blade Ranger. Blade was the chief of Fire and Rescue, and he was going to train and certify Dusty to be a firefighter.

After the morning rush, during which a total of five cow tractors crossed the road, Chug gave the all clear. Mayday, Dottie, Chug, Sparky, and Skipper surrounded Dusty, ready to send him on his way.

"Good luck, Dusty!" shouted Mayday.

"Take it easy out there," added Dottie.

"You can do it, Dusty!" cheered Skipper.

"Wahoo! Good luck!" said Sparky.

Dusty smiled gratefully at his friends, then took off, soaring into the sky. He climbed toward the clouds and flew over miles and miles of golden cornfields. He felt great. But as soon as his torque gauge rose into the yellow zone, his smile faded. He backed off the power and continued to cruise at an average speed.

Dusty enjoyed the long flight to Piston Peak. He passed over the impressively rugged badlands, with the striking rust-colored mountains. He flew over quaint towns and wide-open farmlands. He knew he was getting close when he caught the fresh scent of pine needles drifting up into the air. Finally, he saw a breathtaking forest stretched out below him.

Towering pines, redwoods, and sequoias covered huge mountains. A railway bridge wound its way around the forest. The Piston Peak Railway locomotive came into view, happily puffing and chugging along the track. He blew his whistle when he saw Dusty. Dusty returned the friendly gesture with a dip of his wing.

The park was absolutely magnificent—Dusty was sure it was one of the most beautiful places on earth. He tilted slightly as he zoomed through a hole in the trunk of one majestic sequoia.

When he flew over the main gate, on which a sign read PISTON PEAK NATIONAL PARK, he could see cars and RVs pouring through the entrance. Soon he could see the awe-inspiring V-6 Valley and, in the distance, the magnificent Piston Peak itself. This place was amazing!

The massive, rustic Fusel Lodge was nestled in the V-6 Valley. The hotel was five stories high and had a wide veranda. Planes touched down on a small airstrip, and helicopters landed on balconies. Dusty smiled as he took in the scene. Gasket Geyser sent up a spout of water in front of the lodge as he flew by. A shiny luxury SUV greeted guests as a concierge forklift hovered by his side.

Dusty flew past Piston Peak, spotting deer tractors grazing on the grass below. Finally, the Air Attack Base came into view. There was a small, modest airstrip with corrugated-steel hangars. Dusty landed and rolled to a stop.

The base was oddly quiet except for the faint, tinny

sounds of a song playing out of an old PA speaker. Dusty looked around. Was this really the air attack base?

Patch, a female tug, was cleaning a spot off a window inside a control tower. Windlifter, a massive heavy-lifting helicopter, was grunting as he curled dozens of logs with his hoist. Dipper, a super-scooper plane, was relaxing, using a corrugated steel reflector to sun herself. Maru, a forklift mechanic, dropped a tool on his tire and jumped up and down in pain. Cabbie, a cargo plane, was listening to a ham radio. *These are the firefighters?* Dusty thought.

VROOM! Suddenly, Drip, a wild-natured ATV with a grabber claw, roared off the top of a muddy ridge and flew right over Dusty, nearly colliding with him! Dusty ducked and Drip landed on the other side of the runway.

Another ATV, Dynamite, hurried over, followed by Blackout. Two other ATVs—Avalanche, a mini-bulldozer, and Pinecone—appeared at the top of the ridge.

"Drip! What's the heck's the matter with you? You nearly took off the guy's canopy!" Dynamite said.

"But Blackout said it was okay to go, dude!" Drip said.

"I did?" Blackout asked.

"He did?" Dynamite asked.

"Yeah. He was like, 'It's okay to go, dude.'"

Dusty spoke up. "Uhhh, I'm sorry. I know you're busy, but I'm looking for the Piston Peak Air Attack Base."

"You are there!" said Drip.

They told Dusty they'd heard that a SEAT was coming for training. The gang introduced themselves to Dusty, and Dusty introduced himself. When Dipper heard "Dusty Crophopper," her eyes popped wide open and she raced over to meet him.

"Shut the hangar door! I—I am your biggest fan. I've seen every single one of your races on RSN! Wow, you're smaller than I thought, but that's okay," Dipper said excitedly. She seemed very interested in Dusty, and she eagerly asked what a world-famous racing star was doing in Piston Peak. Dusty explained that he was between races and was getting certified to help out some friends back home. Dipper thought that was really sweet. She giggled nervously when she introduced herself and made it very clear that she was a "Miss" and not a "Mrs." She had a big crush on Dusty.

When Dusty asked for Blade Ranger, the crew told him he was out looking for spot fires. Windlifter, the helicopter, looked up at the sky as the wind blew, and spoke softly and strangely. "The one the Lakota call Haokah beats his drums with the wind to make thunder. With thunder comes lightning. And with lightning . . . comes fire."

"*Oookaaayyyy,*" said Dusty, wondering what the heck Windlifter was talking about.

"Windlifter, stop scaring our guest! I don't hear any drums," Dipper said lightly.

Everyone was quiet as Windlifter slowly turned to the tower speakers, seeming almost hypnotized. Then a blaring siren cut through the silence, and Patch's voice came through the PA: "All aircraft. We've got a report of a wildfire."

Everyone quickly snapped into action, and the ragtag crew became a firefighting team before Dusty's eyes.

"Come on, boys, let's load up!" Maru shouted as he sped out of his hangar. "Patch—drop the needle!" Heavy-metal music blasted out of the little speaker as the team prepared to take on the fire.

"It's an actual fire?" Dusty asked.

"Oh, yeah," shouted Dipper. "Happens all the time. You guys only hear about the big ones."

Dusty watched, bewildered by the swirl of activity as the crew prepared to go out. The smokejumpers clicked into their parachute packs on the side of a hangar and rolled out. Cabbie fired up his engine and lowered his enormous ramp, allowing the smokejumpers to back in. They piled into the plane.

Maru hooked a hose to Dipper and threw a lever, and she filled up with water. Windlifter attached his retardant tank, and the firefighters taxied out to the runway and took off.

Dusty followed excitedly. "I gotta see this!"

Clouds of smoke drifted up from beyond a ridge. Once they got past the ridge, they could see the fire burning up the valley below. Dusty looked down with shock and amazement.

Suddenly, *VROOM!* A fire and rescue helicopter emerged from a column of smoke. He climbed into the air and dove back down as he turned and flipped to release his red retardant on the raging fire below.

"Whoa!" Dusty was beyond impressed. He knew right away that this awesome firefighter had to be Blade.

"All right, mud-droppers, watch your altitude. Too low and you'll spread the embers," Blade commanded.

Blade told the crew what to do and everyone obeyed. He told Dipper where to drop and she went off, diving and releasing her retardant on the edge of the fire. On Blade's command, Windlifter laid retardant on the other side of the fire. Next, Blade ordered Cabbie to open his ramp to get the jumpers on the ground. When Cabbie's back ramp opened, the jumpers rolled forward and peered out the back of the plane.

"Looks good, Cabbie," Dynamite said.

BZZZZ!

The smokejumpers grinned. The loud buzzing noise was accompanied by a green light.

"Let's ride the silk elevator, boys!" Drop said.

"I will never understand why you gravel-crunchers want to jump out of a perfectly good airplane," said Cabbie.

"We're not. We're jumpin' outta *you*!" Dynamite yelled as they hooted and hollered, jumping off the ramp.

The smokejumpers twirled through the air like acrobats, flipping and spinning around, before finally deploying their bright yellow parachutes. The parachutes puffed open and caught the wind, allowing the jumpers to gracefully drift to the ground and land about a hundred yards from the fire. Once down, Dynamite made sure everyone had landed and then radioed Cabbie. "Everyone's down. We're good!"

Cabbie soared off. "Be careful out there!"

Blade told Dynamite to use the creek bed as a barrier to create a fire break. The smokejumpers immediately went to work. Everyone had a specific job to do, and they knew exactly how to do it. Blackout sawed trees, Avalanche pushed debris, Drip lifted a log, and Pinecone raked up brush. They worked together seamlessly, each one performing their task without missing a beat.

Blade spotted several deer tractors scurrying away from the fire as trees fell around them. A burned pine tree cracked and began to fall toward an unsuspecting deer. Blade pitched sideways, opened his side door, and activated a hoist. *ZZZZIP!* The hoist snatched up the deer just as the burning tree smashed to the ground! Blade set the wide-eyed, grateful deer safely on a rocky ledge.

"Awesome!" Dusty said, thrilled.

When Blade noticed Dusty, he was not happy. "Who the—? Get outta this airspace!" he yelled.

Dusty wasn't paying attention and didn't realize how low he was flying. He was very close to the fire.

"Oh! Sorry. Sorry—didn't mean to . . . ," Dusty stammered.

Just then, Dipper swooped in. She didn't see Dusty and dropped a load of retardant right on top of him. *SPLOOSH!* The red retardant covered him from nose to tail.

"Ooooh . . . Uh-oh!" Dipper said.

Dusty, red-faced with retardant, sputtered and wobbled. Blade glared at him.

"Aaaaah! *Heeeeey!* Aaaagh!" Dusty screamed as Maru blasted him with the icy-cold water from the fire hose back at the base. Maru was trying to wash off the retardant.

"That oughta do it," he said with one last blast.

Blade told Dusty to dry off and get back to the lodge with the other tourists.

"Uh . . . I'm not a tourist," said Dusty as Blade rolled away. "I'm the guy—"

"He's the trainee," said Windlifter.

Blade stopped in his tracks, annoyed. *"You're* the SEAT Mayday radioed about? Oh, for the love o'—"

Dipper stepped in and proudly introduced Dusty to Blade. "He's not just *some* SEAT. Seriously? It's *Dusty Crophopper!*"

Dusty was embarrassed. "No, no—it's okay."

Dipper continued. "The champion air racer! Tell him, tell him!"

"Champion. No big deal," Dusty said modestly, looking at the ground.

"He raced all the way around the *world!*" Dipper said enthusiastically.

Dusty suppressed a chuckle. "I did. I did do that. . . ."

Blade stared at Dusty for a moment, unimpressed. "The world wasn't on fire though, was it?" he said, glaring.

"Was the . . . whole world on fire?" Dusty was baffled. "No," he replied.

Blade leaned menacingly toward Dusty. "Maru!" he yelled.

"What?" asked the mechanic.

"Rip off his landing gear," ordered Blade.

"Wait . . . WHAT?" exclaimed Dusty. He didn't like the sound of that. He looked toward Maru, concerned. Maru grinned, revealing his missing tooth. He chuckled evilly as he flipped down his visor and held up a welder, sparks flying.

Inside Maru's cluttered service hangar, racks and workbenches were piled high with old spare parts and equipment. It looked nothing like Dottie's neat and organized garage. Tools, cans of oil, and random parts and pieces of metal were scattered all about. It looked more like a wacky inventor's workshop than a service hangar.

Once Dusty's landing gear was off, Maru welded a set of patched-together pontoons on Dusty.

"Feels pretty weird without the tip tanks," Dusty said.

"Tip tanks? Ha, you couldn't exactly go flying into fire with fuel tanks on your wings. *KABOOM!*" Maru laughed and explained that while the pontoons were old, they would let Dusty scoop water right off the lake.

"Old? You're goofing on me. You got any new ones?" Dusty asked.

"New? Ha! We don't even know what that word means around here. I rebuilt these babies myself.

They're better than new!" Maru finished welding and told Dusty to test them out.

Dusty tried to move across the floor, but the pontoons were clunky and awkward.

"Pop the wheels, genius," Maru said, mocking him.

"Huh? Pop the wheels. . . . Oh!" Dusty looked down. *KACHUNK!* The wheels extended from the pontoons and he was able to roll around. Gaining a few inches was pretty cool—he felt tall!

He rolled over to one of the walls, where Maru had hung photos of Fire and Rescue aircraft. "Hey, you guys have a wall of fame, just like the Jolly Wrenches! So what's the deal? What do you have to do to get your picture up here?"

"Crash."

"Oh," Dusty said solemnly.

"Yep, dangerous work, but that's the job of a firefighter . . . riskin' their lives for people they don't even know." Maru moved equipment onto shelves as he tried to tidy up a bit. "They fly in when others are flyin' out. It takes a special kinda plane."

Dusty looked at the photos of the fallen firefighters with respect and admiration.

The next day, Blade took Dusty to Augerin Canyon to begin training. The narrow canyon was breathtaking as it twisted and curved into the pine-covered forest, following the river. Huge outcroppings of rocks and boulders dotted the landscape. Natural arches stretched across parts of the canyon like strange, jagged bridges.

At the far end of the canyon a narrow road by the river met up with a massive wooden bridge. Whitewall Falls, a mile-high rushing waterfall, thundered down the mountain behind the bridge.

"Fighting wildfires means flying low. That's why we have Augerin Canyon. Our own little obstacle course," Blade said. "All you gotta do is stay below the rim, and when you get to the bridge, fly under and pull out."

"Flying low. No problem," Dusty said. He felt ready.

"Overconfidence. The kind of attitude that can get you killed."

Dusty dove into the canyon and expertly avoided arches and obstacles, showing off his agility.

"Nice flying for a nice day," said Blade. "But a canyon like this will be filled with smoke, airborne debris, and downdrafts. Now let's see you make it under that bridge."

Dusty sped up and headed for the wooden bridge by the falls. He was so focused on the task that for a moment, he completely forgot about his busted gearbox. His face fell when he remembered, and he looked at the torque gauge. It was climbing through the yellow zone, toward the red.

The needle touched red, and the warning light started to flash. Panicking, Dusty pulled up and out of the canyon, easing back on his power. The flashing stopped, and Dusty cleared the rim and joined up with Blade.

"Why'd you pull power?" Blade yelled.

"The bridge. It's too close to the falls!" Dusty said.

"No excuses. If there'd been a downdraft, you'd be dead!"

Next, Blade brought Dusty over to Anchor Lake to learn how to scoop water. The big, shimmering lake was home to an anchor-shaped island, and Dipper was there to demonstrate as Blade and Dusty took in the view. Dusty watched as Dipper flew over trees and dropped down sharply toward Anchor Lake. She gracefully skimmed the surface, scooping up water. Then she climbed back above the trees on the opposite side. She made it look so easy.

Now it was Dusty's turn. He took a deep breath and descended, wobbling nervously.

"Okay, now, you've got a fifty-foot approach, twelve to fifteen seconds to scoop, then fifty feet to climb out. And watch out for the treeline," Blade instructed.

Dusty dropped quickly and skipped across the water, bouncing up and down. He was barely airborne when he met up with the treeline and was unable to avoid it. "Ahhh!" Dusty screamed as his pontoons scraped the trees. Blade frowned.

Later, Dusty went inside the main hangar and listened as Blade lectured about firefighting safety. Maru helped by pointing with a marker to a list on the blackboard, on which SAFETY FIRST was circled.

"And finally, all aircraft must be on the ground thirty minutes after sunset. Flyin' low at night is the fastest way to get your picture on the wall," Blade said.

Dusty listened carefully and took notes.

Next, it was time for Dusty to practice dropping flame retardant. He would need to line up and aim before dropping the retardant to hit the target. Big, flaming wooden barrels were set up on the tarmac as practice targets.

"Height. Speed. Topography. Accuracy is everything," Blade said.

Dusty took a deep breath and dove over the flaming barrels. He aimed and released his retardant . . . extinguishing only one of the barrels.

"Too early!" barked Blade.

Dusty tried again, and this time his retardant sprinkled down weakly. It didn't hit even one barrel!

"Too high."

On his third attempt, the drop knocked all the

barrels over . . . but they were still lit!

"Too low," said Blade. "Those crops o' yours—they die a lot?"

Dusty didn't respond. Training was definitely a lot tougher than he had thought it would be.

Blade brought Dusty back to Augerin Canyon for another shot at making it under the bridge. Poised and ready, Dusty focused as he pushed power, determined to get to the other side. He had to gain enough speed to fly under the bridge and then straight back up into the sky before hitting the falls.

"You need to be alert, keep calm, think clearly, and act decisively," Blade said. Dusty was almost there when his warning light came on.

Discouraged, Dusty slowed his engine and pulled up early, just before reaching the bridge. It was starting to get late, so another attempt at the bridge would have to wait until tomorrow.

That night, Dusty was exhausted but slept restlessly. In the middle of the night he felt like someone was watching him. When he opened his eyes, he was startled. "Guh!" Dusty yelped when he saw Dipper's adoring eyes peering through the hangar door. It was creepy! As soon as she knew she was caught, she quickly ducked out of sight.

The next day, Dusty tried to conquer the bridge in Augerin Canyon once again. Determined, he headed for the long wooden bridge, and then—*FLASH! FLASH! FLASH!* Warning light again.

"Approach looks good. Now go to max torque. Really push it. Redline it! Redline it!" Blade yelled.

Dusty slowed his engine to make the warning light stop and pulled up before making it under the bridge.

"If you don't push it, you're not gonna make it, and you won't be certified," Blade said sternly.

Dusty was really frustrated. He felt that he was completely failing as a trainee. Then he noticed smoke on the horizon, coming up from the forest. He grinned at Blade and zoomed toward the smoke. Dusty was determined to do *something* right. He dove, focused, and got ready to make a drop. He aimed and released the water right at the base of the column of smoke!

"Bull's-eye!" Dusty said triumphantly.

Blade came over to see what Dusty had done. The two looked down to see a soaking-wet family of four RVs around a soggy campfire. The two kid RVs cried as their mother tried to comfort them. The dad RV scowled up at Blade and Dusty.

"Good job," said Blade. "You just saved those folks from a nice vacation."

Dusty couldn't even look at Blade, he was so humiliated.

Later that evening, Dusty rolled into his hangar dirty, exhausted, and disappointed in himself. The radio crackled to life. "Propwash Junction to Dusty. Come in, Dusty." It was Chug! Dusty pushed down on the pedal and spoke into the radio.

"Hey, Chug!"

"How's it going, Duster?"

"This is tougher than I thought, but it's so good to hear from you."

Skipper, Dottie, Mayday, and Sparky were on the other end, too. His friends were calling with some exciting news.

"We got the gearbox!" Chug said proudly.

"Are you kidding me?"

Sparky told Dusty that someone they knew in California had the gearbox and was going to ship it out tonight! They would get it in a couple of days. Dusty couldn't believe what he was hearing. It was like an enormous weight had been lifted off his wings.

"Couple days? Wow. Thanks! That's . . . that's the best news. Just what I needed to hear right now," Dusty said gratefully.

"Hey, Dusty! Listen to my new siren!" Mayday said. He took a big breath and squinted while trying to force out his siren sound. *SQuuuuuEEEEEEEEEEeeeee!* It sounded like a big, old balloon slowly letting out air. The room was silent as Mayday waited for a big response.

"Yeah . . . I haven't actually hooked up his siren yet," said Dottie, cringing.

Just then, Patch's voice came over the PA. "Superintendent Spinner has entered the base!"

Dusty said goodbye to his friends and went outside to see what was going on.

Maru was washing Dipper and Windlifter. Dusty asked him what was up.

"Eh—park superintendent," Maru said, clearly unimpressed.

It was obvious to Dusty that his new friends were not fans of the park superintendent.

Cad Spinner rolled up to the base, honking his horn obnoxiously. *Honk, honk! Beep, beep!* "Park superintendent coming. I sign your paychecks. Anyone gonna greet me? Yes, you are!"

"I got some oil pans to change," Maru said unenthusiastically as he rolled off.

Blade approached Cad. "What do you want, Cad?" he asked with an aggravated sigh.

"Listen—do I like driving all around and over here and up here just to complain? Answer: No, I don't. But I heard from some campers that one of your staff soaked 'em with that . . . red . . . fire . . . phosphorescent stuff . . . that you use. The deodorant."

Dusty rolled forward to apologize, but Blade cut him off.

"The team needs to train," said Blade firmly. "There's gonna be some mud spilled along the way." Dusty was surprised that Blade had come to his defense.

Then Cad recognized Dusty and he didn't want to talk about the unhappy campers anymore. "Are you kidding me?" Cad rolled up to Dusty and stared at him. "Blade, you're hiding a world-famous racer right here at Piston Peak!"

Dusty grinned, embarrassed.

"Rip-SLING-aaa!" Cad shouted.

"Uh, it's Crophopper," said Dusty.

"Crop-HOP-aaa!"

Cad asked Dusty what he was doing in Piston Peak, then interrupted when Dusty tried to answer. He wanted Dusty to go to the big grand reopening party for the Fusel Lodge. He said there would be a lot of VIPs—Very Important Planes—attending. "How would you like to rub tires with the secretary of the interior of the United States of America? I smell a photo op! FLASH! *Cha-ching.* Ya gotta do it. Come on! Heh heh . . ."

Blade started talking to Cad about safety. He was irritated with Cad for his lack of concern. "You've packed too many 'happy campers' into the park, and way too many into that lodge," he said.

"We've got a structural fire engine down there protecting it," said Cad, referring to Engine Pulaski, a fire truck who worked by the lodge.

"This isn't just about protecting the lodge," Blade explained. "There's low humidity, a lot o' dead wood, and we're short on resources."

Dipper leaned in and whispered to Dusty, "He got the parks service to shift eighty percent of our budget to his lodge-restoration project."

"This base is held together with baling wire and duct tape. Maru had to rebuild that ol' tower himself!" Blade said, gesturing toward the tower.

"S'better than new!" Maru proudly shouted from beside it.

Cad didn't seem to care. He was only concerned about the weekend's reopening festivities. His cell phone rang and he raised his antenna to answer it. The others watched, annoyed, as he took the call.

"Cad. You've got thirty seconds, go. . . . No, no, no, I don't care how much it costs. Get the crystal glasses. . . ." Cad rolled off to finish his conversation, and then returned to the crew. He reminded Dusty to go to the party.

"Can you believe it? Dusty Cropslinger! He's even more famous than you, Blazin' Blade!" Cad said as he drove off. Without another word, Blade huffed and rolled toward his hangar. Confused, Dusty turned to Dipper and Windlifter.

"Blazin' Blade?" Dusty asked.

"SHHH!" Dipper said quickly.

"What?"

"SHH! SHH! SHH!"

"I just said Blazin' Blade."

Windlifter and Dipper shushed Dusty again. Once Blade was out of earshot, Windlifter spoke quietly. "Tonight. Main hangar. Tell no one. Especially Blade."

12

That night, the moon cast a silvery glow over the air attack base. All was calm and still as Dusty quietly rolled over to the main hangar, eager for answers. He waited in front until a peephole opened.

"Password," Maru whispered through the opening.

Dusty was confused. "Password? You didn't tell—"

"Shhh. Shhh," Maru interrupted.

Dusty tried again, whispering this time. "You didn't tell me a password."

"It's 'inferno,'" Maru said dramatically. Then he smiled, revealing his missing tooth.

"Oh. Okay."

Maru waited as his smile turned to a frown.

"Oh . . . inferno," Dusty whispered.

Maru slid the peephole firmly shut and opened the hangar doors.

Inside, Dipper, Windlifter, and Cabbie were sitting around an old rear-projection television. The smokejumpers rolled up close to the screen and fought over where to sit. Everyone excitedly grabbed cans of oil and got comfortable.

"Park it over here, Dust Storm," said Dipper sweetly. "Saved you a spot."

Warily, Dusty rolled over to Dipper. She scooted close, cuddling against him. Then she slowly and shyly put her wing around him.

Maru held up an old videotape with the title *Howard the Truck*.

Dusty had no idea what was going on. "*Howard the Truck*? You invited me here to watch—"

"Dude, dude, dude! Judge not a video by its cover," Drip said.

Maru slid the tape out of the case to reveal its white

After winning the Wings Around The Globe Rally,
Dusty Crophopper is an air-racing legend!

Fans around the world admire Dusty.

During a routine flight above Propwash Junction,
Dusty experiences engine problems.

Dusty makes an emergency landing and accidentally crashes
into the Fill 'n' Fly, causing it to explode!

Skipper, Mayday, Chug, and Dusty pull the water tower down to put out the fire.

Mayday, the town's fire engine, is touched when Dusty tells him he will train to become a second firefighter.

Dusty's friends wish him luck as he takes off for Piston Peak
National Park to begin his firefighting training!

When Dusty arrives at the Piston Peak Air Attack Base,
he meets Blackout, Dynamite, Windlifter, and Dipper.
They're real firefighters!

Avalanche and Pinecone clear brush and debris from
the front lines of forest fires.

Blade is the leader of the Piston Peak Air Attack Team and
a veteran fire-and-rescue helicopter. He extinguishes fires
by dropping fire retardant.

Dipper is a super-scooper who can skim lakes to collect water.

Maru is the mechanic at the air base. He can fix anything!

Dusty enjoys hanging out with his new firefighting friends.

Blade isn't sure Dusty has what it takes to be a firefighter.

Taking shelter from a fire in an old mine shaft, Blade shields Dusty from a firestorm.

Dusty realizes that just like becoming a racer, becoming a firefighter is hard work.

homemade label: EPISODE 17: "DISCO INFERNO" was scribbled on it in blue marker. Maru pushed the tape into the VCR, and it whirred to life when he hit the play button.

After an old commercial for the law offices of Larry H. Parkinglot, a disco beat began to play over a black screen. Two blue-and-gold California Helicopter Patrol copters appeared in the sky over a big city. The snappy theme song began as the show's title, *ChoPs*, appeared on the screen. The two stars grinned as their names popped up: "BLAZIN'" BLADE RANGER AND NICK "LOOP'N" LOPEZ!

"Hold on," Dusty said, trying to understand what he was seeing. "Blade was a TV star?"

"One hundred thirty-nine episodes of law-breakin' love," Dipper said, giggling.

The smokejumpers, eager to enjoy the show, shushed everyone. On the screen, a boot was being clamped onto a five-spoke mag wheel.

"Good move, partner," Blazin' Blade said with a wink and a smile.

The show was pretty cheesy, but Blade and Nick were the heroes and they had a lot of charm. In the "Disco Inferno" episode, they busted a surly-looking muscle car and then got called to a burning high-rise, where a pink Ford Pinto was screaming from a balcony.

When Blazin' Blade activated his hoist to save the Pinto, everyone in the hangar yelled, "Hoist!" and then simultaneously slurped from their oil cans. Dusty could see that this was a tradition with the crew.

Once the show was over, the credits rolled by as the theme music played again.

"This show stinks," said Cabbie.

"I'm with Cabbie," Windlifter said.

The smokejumpers got defensive and started yelling at Windlifter and Cabbie. They loved *ChoPs*!

"What are you talking about?" said Dynamite. "This show's the best."

"Are you crazy?" Pinecone glared at Windlifter and Cabbie. "There is not a better show in all creation, if you ask me."

Drip jumped in. "Take it back. You did not say that. Go. Get out. Leave the room."

Dusty couldn't even form an opinion about it. He had so many questions. "If Blade was such a big TV star, what's he doing here?" he asked.

"I don't know," said Drip. "It's a mysterious mystery."

The jumpers had all kinds of theories, but nobody knew for sure.

"Whatever the reason is, it's his business, and we're not askin'," said Dynamite firmly.

Later that night, bright streaks of lightning cracked across the dark sky as a storm hit Piston Peak. Dusty peered out of his hangar and saw Blade perched on an overlook, keeping watch on the sky and the valley beyond. Dusty could see how important firefighting was to Blade. He took his job very seriously.

The next morning, the siren blared across the base, alerting the crew. Patch's voice sounded urgent on the PA as he announced that the lightning had caused multiple forest fires. Maru got busy right away, mixing up flame retardant.

The smokejumpers sped across the tarmac and loaded into Cabbie after he lowered his gate.

"Lightnin' storm started a whole slew o' spot fires, and they've merged," said Blade. "This is a big one."

What made matters worse was that the wind was

causing the fire to spread rapidly. Blade ordered Dipper and Windlifter to load up. He told Dusty to wait in the hangar.

"What?" Dusty asked, disappointed.

"Blade, Dusty's been practicing so hard," Dipper said.

"He's not certified," Blade said.

"We need every plane we've got," said Windlifter.

"I want to help," Dusty pleaded.

Blade thought for a moment, narrowed his eyes, and called to Maru. "Load him up." Then he took off.

Maru rolled up and snapped a picture of Dusty with his camera.

"What was that for?"

"The wall," Maru said bluntly.

At the fire, the smokejumpers were busy at work, doing what they did best. Blackout sawed through a thick log, and Drip dragged it out of the way. Pinecone raked the brush into a pile, and Avalanche pushed the pile off to the side. Dipper flew overhead, releasing retardant on the fire.

"Dipper, come left one wingspan on your next drop. Champ, tag on and extend. Split load," Blade ordered.

"Copy that," said Dusty.

Dusty dove and lined up for his drop, focusing on the target. He concentrated, aimed, and dropped.

"Too high!" Blade said angrily. "It all dispersed. Windlifter, finish off that ridge."

Dusty huffed in frustration. He was trying his best—why had he missed his target?

On the ground, Dynamite eyed the ridge, sensing a problem. The wind suddenly shifted, and the smoke started blowing in the other direction. Then the fire jumped the line and ignited the trees behind the jumpers! "Pull back! Pull back! Let's go right now!" Dynamite yelled to the other smokejumpers.

With embers blowing all around them, the smokejumpers turned away from the fire as it quickly moved toward them. Dynamite led the jumpers to a dry creek bed. They thought they could find safety there, but then there was a sudden loud *CRACK* as a massive burning pine tree fell to the ground, blocking their path.

Dynamite radioed Blade. "The wind shifted. The fire jumped the line."

"Can you make it to your safety zone?" asked Blade.

"No. No good. Our escape route is blocked. We need a drop," replied Dynamite.

Blade called Dipper, but Dusty responded first. "I see 'em. I've got it!" he said, determined to help out.

Dusty soared above the smokejumpers. Concentrating, he aimed and released his retardant . . . right on target! Dusty had finally done it! The flames were extinguished.

"We're clear! Let's move!" Dynamite called to the other jumpers. They were safe.

"That's my Dustmuffin!" Dipper yelled proudly.

"Champ, load and return," Blade said. "We still got a lot o' work to do today."

"Copy that," Dusty said with a big grin on his face. He had finally done something right!

The crew worked hard to contain the fire, and Dusty continued to do his best to help. It was a really long day, but at the end of it, Dusty felt great.

Once the sun finally started to set, the crew returned to the base, exhausted and covered in soot.

"Dynamite just reported in—they're gonna camp out tonight and mop it up tomorrow," said Patch over the PA.

Maru asked Cabbie how the fire was looking.

"We got that sucker boxed in," replied Cabbie.

"Nice work!" Maru complimented him.

"So . . . that's it?" asked Dusty.

Dipper explained to Dusty that now that the fire was contained, the jumpers would continue to work on it until it was completely out. "You did a great job out there, sweet seat," she said sincerely.

"Thanks. I saw the jumpers were in trouble, so—"

Blade rolled by. "You broke formation in a crowded airspace," he said firmly. "Could've been *you* spread all over the woods instead o' *retardant*. Don't go plannin' your certification party yet, Champ." Blade rolled off, leaving Dusty feeling as charred as the burned-up pine trees.

"Ah, man," Dusty said with a sigh.

"C'mon, that's just Blade's way of sayin' 'good job,'" Dipper said gently.

SHOOOOM! SHOOOOM! SHOOOOM! Several big private jets flew right over their heads.

"Whoa," said Dipper. "That was low."

Windlifter said it had to be Cad's VIPs arriving for the big grand-opening party.

Dusty had completely forgotten—the party was later that night. "Hey, we should go!" he said.

"A second date?" Dipper said with a huge smile.

"Ah, I kinda meant all of us. You, me, Windlifter, just everybody."

"Oh . . . okay. No, no, you're right. I should get to know your friends," Dipper said.

"But they're *your* friends," Dusty said, confused.

Dipper chuckled. "Yeah, I guess. Let's not bicker."

Dusty looked at Windlifter, bewildered. Windlifter just shrugged.

The Fusel Lodge looked absolutely gorgeous against the night sky. Gasket Geyser erupted every now and then, adding a dramatic touch to the scenery.

Inside, the lodge was buzzing with activity as excited vehicles entered the luxurious lobby. Bellhop forklifts swiftly rolled by, wheeling towering racks of luggage and leading visitors to their rooms. It was clear that Cad had spared no expense in restoring the old place. Magnificent chandeliers sparkled as they hung from the high ceiling, and a fire crackled in the giant stone fireplace, warming the cars lounging in solid oak rocking chairs. The train tracks curved in, right behind the check-in area, allowing the train to drop off passengers inside.

Dusty, Dipper, Windlifter, and Maru entered the lodge, still covered in soot and grime from fighting the fire all day. They certainly stood out against the elegant lodge.

"Whoa. Look at this place!" Dusty said in awe. He had never seen anything like it.

"It's so beautiful," said Dipper.

"So this is where our budget went," said Maru bitterly.

Dipper noticed a bride and groom drive by, obviously on their honeymoon. "They do weddings here, did you know that?" she asked Dusty cheerfully.

His eyes popped and he said nothing.

When André, the stuffy concierge forklift, noticed the crew standing there dripping mud all over the marble floor, he clapped to call over three little vacuum cleaners. They rolled out quickly and quietly, bouncing here and there as they covered every inch of the mess. They cleaned it up in a flash, then rolled away, disappearing as quickly as they had entered.

The train puffed into the station and more guests poured out, including the one Cad was most excited about: the secretary of the interior. Cad waited eagerly to greet him with a welcome party of forklifts. "Welcome, Mr. Secretary, to the grand reopening weekend of the magnificent Fusel Lodge," Cad said, rolling right up to him.

"It's a pleasure to be here, Spinner," the secretary replied.

"And is it a pleasure to see you, sir? Yes, it is," said Cad as he led the secretary toward the main lobby.

"So now, what's this I hear about a fire?" asked the secretary.

"Uh, fire?"

Engine Pulaski, the lodge's fire truck, and his assistant, Rake, rolled by. "The Whitewall Fire is contained, sir," said Pulaski, in response to the secretary's question.

"Right," Cad said.

"It's under control," Pulaski added.

Cad quickly jumped in. "It's absolutely under control. Thank you, uh . . ."

"Engine Pulaski, sir."

"Whoski?"

"Pulaski."

Cad quickly changed the subject and went back to addressing the secretary. "Anyway, right this way, sir. And if there are any other questions you have for me, please—I am your man."

"I do have several questions. Tell me, how is the park's indigenous wildlife population?" the secretary asked.

"The what?" Once again, Cad seemed to be caught off guard. He obviously didn't know the answer to the secretary's question.

"The wildlife."

"The wildlife? Well, if you come to the party tonight, there'll be plenty of party animals," Cad said with a laugh, trying to make a joke.

"I see. Yes," the secretary said, unimpressed.

Ol' Jammer, an old tour bus and park ranger, had overheard the secretary's question. "The deer population is steady. And we've had a healthy increase in the number of red-propped balsa thrush," he said.

"Glad to hear it. Say, I didn't quite catch your name. . . ."

"Ranger Jammer, sir. Seventy-two years at Piston Peak."

"Pleased to meet you, Jammer."

"It's a true pleasure to meet you, sir," replied Jammer.

Cad was clearly irritated that Jammer was befriending the secretary.

Nearby, Dusty and Dipper were admiring the beauty of the lodge.

"Wow, look at that ice sculpture!" said Dipper as she rolled up beside an intricate model of the lodge that had been chiseled from a block of ice. "This could be our room . . . if we were little tiny pieces of ice."

Suddenly, Dusty heard his name being called out and a fan appeared before him, snapping pictures with his cell phone.

"Huh? Whoa, whoa," said Dusty, blinded by the flashes.

"My buddies are never gonna believe this. Oh, oh, oh! Hey, do my voice mail!" exclaimed the fan.

"Your voice mail? Uh . . . ," Dusty said, confused.

The fan held up his phone. "Do it!" he yelled.

"What? Oh—hi, this is Dusty Crophop—"

"World racing champion—" the fan interrupted.

Dusty cleared his throat. "World racing champion. Please leave a message at the beep."

"Now beep," the fan demanded.

"What?"

"Do it."

"Beeeeep."

"Ha, ha! That was awesome!" the fan said excitedly.

Then Cad spotted Dusty and rushed toward him. He was eager to get away from Jammer, who was still chatting with the secretary.

"Dusty, superstar, you have to meet the secretary of the interior!" Cad said. Then he leaned in close and whispered, "I'm up for a promotion. You understand, you're upwardly mobile, right? Course you are, you're a *plane*."

"Uh, okay. Sure," said Dusty, wondering what exactly Cad expected him to do.

Then Cad noticed someone else who was famous— Boat Reynolds, a boat with a manly mustache. He quickly left Dusty, rushing off to try to meet the famous actor.

A nice old RV couple, Winnie and Harvey, approached Dusty. They had honeymooned in the park fifty years before and were celebrating their wedding anniversary. They seemed to be as much in love as they must have been when they got married. Harvey asked Dusty for help. He was looking at a map of the park on the wall, trying to figure out where they'd had their first kiss.

"Aw, that is so sweet!" said Dipper. She leaned into a confused Dusty and said, "You don't do things like that anymore."

"There was a bridge, and a magnificent waterfall, and . . . you," Harvey said, looking lovingly at Winnie.

"I love you, Harvey," Winnie said, smiling at him.

"Hey, y'know, that sounds like Augerin Canyon," Dusty said.

"Yeah, that's right! Anger Canyon," said Harvey.

"By Upper Whitewall Falls!" continued Dusty.

"By Whitewash Falls! See? I told you I knew where it was," Harvey said to Winnie.

"Hey, in honor of your anniversary, why don't you join us?" asked Dipper.

Dusty chimed in and offered to buy them a can of oil.

"Oh, thank you, dear," said Winnie.

Windlifter, Dipper, Winnie, Harvey, Dusty, and Maru

went out to the veranda. They sat around a table with a small fire pit in the center and drank cans of oil as they chatted and enjoyed the warmth of the fire. Dusty felt a little like he was back home at Honkers Sports Bar. It was really nice hanging out and relaxing with his new friends.

"You know, Dusty, I've seen a lot of trainees come through here. And you, well…you just might have what it takes," said Maru.

Dusty smiled. "Thanks, Maru."

"Maybe you found yourself a second career!" said Harvey. "I worked as a taco truck, sold car wash curtain rings for a while. Then I got into RV tire sales. Winnie here was my showroom model."

"That's how we met," said Winnie.

"Awww," said Dusty, smiling.

"You know, Dusty, maybe this firefighting thing will be a second career for you!" said Harvey.

"Oh yeah! This is a second career for all of us," Dipper said. "Windlifter was a lumberjack, Cabbie was in the military—and me, well, I hauled cargo up in Anchorage." She nodded. "Yup, a lot of guys up in Anchorage. I was beatin' 'em off with a stick!"

Dusty wondered . . . he had been a crop duster and then a racer. Maybe Harvey was right. Firefighting could be his next career.

"Hey, big whirlybird," Harvey said to Windlifter. "You haven't said much. How about a toast?"

"Uh, Windlifter's not really much for speeches," said Dipper quickly.

Windlifter, who was chanting to himself, suddenly stopped. "A toast to Coyote!" he said. The firelight cast an eerie glow around him as he continued solemnly. "It was he who drove all day and all night to the base of Bright Mountain. With much difficulty, he climbed the mountain to obtain fire, and brought it down to the first vehicles. But in so doing, he burned his tires. And when Coyote saw his blackened tires, he thought they were his favorite snack . . . AND HE ATE THEM!"

Everyone gasped—except Maru, who just smiled.

Windlifter continued. "For he knew they were still full of life. And it was in this way he let go of the old and renewed himself like fire renews the earth."

Everyone sat silently, glancing around at each other for a moment. No one had ever heard a story like Windlifter's before. They were all speechless.

Finally, Dusty broke the silence. "I'm just gonna say it. You had me up until the part where he *eats his own tires.*"

"Best toast ever, Windlifter," Maru said happily, raising his can. "Cheers!"

"CHEERS," everyone said, clinking their oil cans together.

Early the next morning, Dusty was still asleep when the sunlight began to stream through the window of his hangar. The radio crackled and squawked to life, waking him. "Propwash Junction to Dusty. Come in, Dusty." Skipper's voice sounded far away through the scratchy old radio.

Tired, Dusty rolled backward, knocking into a pile of boxes. He yawned and said, "Hey, Skip."

"Come in, Dust—"

Oops. Dusty realized he'd forgotten to step on the pedal. He rolled onto the pedal, holding it down, and tried again. "Hey, Skipper. What's up? Oh—did the gearbox come in?"

Back in Dottie's garage, Dottie, Sparky, Chug, and Skipper looked somber. An open parts box sat on a bench beside them. Skipper fumbled for an answer.

"Wh-what?" Dusty asked, begging for information.

The gang shared a sad look. No one wanted to be the bearer of bad news. Finally, Chug's voice crackled through the radio. "It was the wrong one. The crate . . . it was mislabeled. We've called every parts supplier, repair shop, and junkyard in the country. Nobody has your gearbox."

Dusty shut his eyes. It took a moment for the news to sink in.

"Dusty?" Skipper said gently.

"I'm here" was all Dusty could say.

"I'm sorry," said Skipper.

Dusty fought back tears. For a moment, he was too

disappointed to talk. "I gotta go. Thanks." He lifted off the radio pedal and sadly looked at his torque gauge. What was he supposed to do? He felt as worthless as the junk scattered about the hangar.

Suddenly, the blast of the siren rang out across the base, and Patch's voice came blaring over the PA. "All aircraft, we've got two wildfires—I repeat, two wildfires: one east of Coil Springs, the other just west of Whitewall Rapids. Use extreme caution. They are really rippin'."

Dusty stayed completely still as he heard the crew getting ready to fight the fire. He felt paralyzed by the disappointing news about the gearbox.

Just then, Maru burst into Dusty's hangar, startling him. "Get this—Cad's fancy-jet VIPs flew in too low over the burn area last night, blew embers in all directions."

Dusty had no reaction and remained motionless. Then Blade rolled up alongside Maru and called loudly to Dusty, "Champ, let's load and go!"

Smoke billowed into the sky as two massive fires burned on either side of V-6 Valley. The fires were moving forward fast, getting closer and closer to each other. If they joined up, the resulting fire would likely burn down the entire forest.

"All right, mud-droppers. Fire broke containment and split in two," Blade said. "Windlifter, you and Dipper take the Coil Springs fire. Me and the SEAT will take Whitewall Rapids."

Windlifter and Dipper peeled off to the left as Blade and Dusty went to the right.

The mountainside was ablaze, and the flames were rapidly growing and spreading. As Blade and Dusty crested the mountain, they could see the fire climbing toward the lodge.

Blade radioed Maru, "It's worse than we thought." He ordered Maru to call the lodge and tell them to evacuate immediately. "That fire is about four hours from their front door."

Maru radioed Cad right away, but Cad didn't want to hear it.

"I've been working on this lodge for five years. I'm not gonna evacuate *now* just to be 'safe'!" yelled Cad.

Maru pleaded with Cad, telling him he had to get everyone out right away. He made it very clear that they would be in danger if they stayed in the lodge.

"Why am I talking to you?" barked Cad. "Where's Blade?"

"Oh, he's out back sippin' a motorjito. Where do ya think he is? He's out fightin' the fire!" Maru yelled back.

In the forest, waves of flames ripped through the

pines at an incredibly fast rate as the fire advanced up a ridge. Blade and Dusty flew toward it side by side.

Blade talked to Dusty about the plan of attack. "I'll drop, then you tag on and extend. And make it a split load. That way we can double up and widen it downwind of the ridge for structure protection. There's not much time, so we need to move fast. Copy that?"

Dusty wasn't listening. He was distracted by the news about his gearbox. He focused on his torque gauge and listened closely to the sound of his engine. Blade's words were not reaching him. Chug's and Dottie's voices echoed in his head.

"If you push yourself into the red, you'll crash," Dottie had said.

"Nobody has your gearbox," Chug had said.

"Copy that? Hey!" Blade yelled, and Dusty snapped to attention.

"Huh?"

"You copy that?"

"Yeah—yes. Copy that," Dusty replied, recovering.

Blade dropped a line of retardant in front of the fire. Dusty followed, and then dropped all of his retardant down on the fire as well.

"You gotta be kidding me. Was that your whole tank?" Blade yelled.

"Yeah."

"You just wasted all of it!"

"I was just following your orders," said Dusty.

"I said split load! We were going to make a secondary line to protect that lodge," shouted Blade.

Dusty brushed Blade off and said everything would be fine. He said he could just reload at the lake, and then he began to arc toward the water.

Blade went after him. "Negative. Return to base," he said.

"What? There's no time. Let's just get this fire out." Dusty said, dismissing Blade's orders.

"Hey, you need to listen to me!"

"I'll be fine!" Dusty yelled as he continued toward the water.

Blade followed him. "These crosswinds are too strong. Return to base!" he yelled.

But Dusty refused to listen. "If we're gonna get this fire out, I've gotta reload!"

"Pull up! Now!" Blade commanded.

"No, I can do this!" Dusty said, approaching the

lake. When he touched its choppy surface, he bounced up and down wildly, like a stone skipping across the water.

"PULL UP!" Blade shouted.

Dusty's prop hit the lake, and water sprayed everywhere. He tried to start his engine, but it wheezed and choked. "I've taken in too much water," he said. "My engine stalled." Dusty was stuck as he helplessly started to drift down the rapids and straight toward Whitewall Falls.

18

"**G**et your engine started so you can keep your pontoons facing downstream," Blade called. "I'll get ahead of you."

The rapids dragged Dusty down the river, but he still didn't want to listen to Blade. "I'll get out on my own," he said.

"Really? How you plannin' on doing that?" Blade said, annoyed, as he followed Dusty from above. "Hang on. I'm gonna pull you to shore." He lowered his hoist and swung it toward Dusty but missed.

Dusty tried to start his engine again and again, but it kept stalling. He didn't know what to do. He was helpless, drifting down the rapids like a toy boat.

"Are you all right?" Blade called.

"I'm okay," said Dusty, his voice shaking.

"There's too much coverage. I'll get you at the next clearing," Blade called, flying past.

"Ouch!" Dusty yelped as he banged into a log. The river was moving quickly, knocking him this way and that. Dusty had no control over what was happening or where he was going. Blade waited in a clearing, ahead of Dusty. When Dusty approached, Blade tossed his hoist down. But Dusty got caught between some rocks underwater and stopped moving. He was stuck. Blade's hoist missed again, falling into the river.

"Blade . . . ," Dusty called, partially submerged, with the water creeping up around him.

Finally, Dusty broke free from the rocks and screamed as he was pulled down the rapids again. Blade attempted to fly forward, but he couldn't move—his hoist was caught on a fallen tree.

"Blade! Blade!" Dusty desperately called out as he

continued to float downstream.

"You need to start your engine," Blade shouted. "You've got clear water. You can take off before the falls!"

Dusty paused. He was scared.

"It's your only chance!" yelled Blade.

Whitewall Falls was just ahead and coming up fast. Dusty tried to start his engine again—and it worked! "Got it! I'm good," he called.

Blade tugged on his hoist, trying to free it, but it was still firmly wedged beneath the giant fallen tree. "Now redline it!" Blade called to Dusty.

Dusty managed to get a little lift, but his pontoons were still in the water. "Push your engine!" Blade yelled.

Dusty pushed harder and watched his torque gauge near the red zone. Even with his pontoons in the water and the falls quickly approaching, he could only focus on his gauge. Blade continued to yell at Dusty, begging him to redline it. Then Dusty's warning light flashed. He panicked, let off the power, and lost his lift. Whitewall Falls was right in front of him! Dusty clipped a rock and spun right into the massive waterfall!

WHOOSH-CLANK! Blade's hoist hooked Dusty in

a flash. Blade strained as he lifted Dusty up and out of the falls. *SMASH!* Dusty shrieked as he crashed right through a burning tree branch.

When they finally reached the ground and caught their breath, Blade yelled at Dusty for not redlining his engine. "What were you thinking? When I tell you to do something, you do it!" Then Blade eyed the fire, looking very worried. It was ripping through the forest and getting closer to them.

"What? What's wrong?" Dusty asked.

"This ain't good. Head down that path. Follow me." Blade and Dusty flew off.

Blade led Dusty to an old mineshaft tucked into a hillside. Fallen timber and burning debris surrounded the mine, but it was the safest place for them to be. "Champ, come on!" Blade called. "In here!"

Dusty didn't want to go inside. He thought they would run out of air and suffocate. "No—no, you go on. I'll keep moving," Dusty said as he turned down the path. The ground vibrated as burning trees fell in the distance, pounding the earth.

Blade landed right in front of Dusty, blocking his path. He stared him right in the eyes. "What are you doing? You can't outrun the fire," he said.

"You know what, I'll find my way out," said Dusty.

"Like you found your way out of the rapids," Blade said.

"I didn't want to push my engine—"

"You didn't *want* to? This isn't about you. This is about life and death! You need to follow orders!" Blade was furious. "I told you to split load—you dropped it all! I told you not to reload on the lake—you did it anyway! I told you to redline it—you pulled power! You don't have what it takes! You don't!"

"Fine! I never wanted to be a firefighter anyway!"

"Then go back to racing! Go win yourself another trophy—champ!"

"I can't! My gearbox is busted! All right? That's why I pulled power! I'm never gonna race again!" Dusty was exhausted and miserable. He was so overcome with disappointment and sadness that he didn't even feel like himself anymore.

"Life doesn't always go the way you expect it," Blade said with understanding. "But you came here to be a firefighter. If you give up today, think of all the lives you won't save tomorrow." He paused. Then he asked

Dusty: "So, what are you going to do?"

Blade's words washed over Dusty as he stood there amid the rising smoke, falling embers, and ash. He thought for a moment and then slowly entered the mine. Blade looked back at the encroaching flames and followed.

The mine wasn't very deep. Dusty rolled back as far as he could go, and Blade rolled behind him, but there wasn't enough room for both of them. Blade remained half exposed at the entrance.

The terrifying roar and crackle of the forest flames grew louder. Soon smoke began to fill the mineshaft as flames danced across its entrance. Burning embers fell, and Dusty shut his eyes. He had never been so frightened.

Ahhh! A beam collapsed, scraping Dusty's side and partially tearing off his #7 racing decal. Flames clawed, trying to get inside the mine, but Blade blocked them as best he could. The heat caused the paint on his side to bubble and blister, but he didn't budge. Blade stood firm in the entryway, shielding Dusty from the flames.

19

Back outside the Fusel Lodge, Cad was beaming as he stood next to a tarp and spoke to a big crowd. Guests and staff members were there, as was the secretary of the interior. They were all waiting for Cad to unveil a commemorative plaque for the lodge.

Smoke appeared on the horizon, but Cad wasn't about to let that distract him from his big moment. "Is it a beautiful day here at Piston Peak Park? Yes, it is," he said, smiling.

Off to the side, Engine Pulaski argued with André, the concierge. "It is my understanding that Blade has ordered an evacuation. The safety of the tourists is at stake! I need to talk to the superintendent. He must be made aware of the magnitude and urgency of the situation," Pulaski urged.

Cad noticed and glanced back at the crowd, smiling big. He laughed and excused himself. Annoyed, he sped over to Pulaski. "Am I giving a speech? Yes, I am, Penewski."

"No, sir, Pulaski," Pulaski said.

"Papooski."

"Pulaski."

"Patooski."

"Name's Pulaski."

"That what I said. We're saying the same thing."

Pulaski had had enough. "With all due respect, Superintendent Spinner, the smoke over the ridge is growing closer!"

"Perhaps we should turn on the roof sprinklers?" suggested André.

Cad couldn't be bothered with the fire at the moment.

But Pulaski was insistent. "We must evacuate."

"Evacuate, yes, yes!" André agreed.

Just then, Ol' Jammer rolled up. "Listen to 'em, Cad. They're right."

"Come on, Spinner! Let's see that plaque," the secretary of the interior called from the crowd. None of the guests had noticed the fire yet.

"Right away, sir!"

Pulaski told Cad to cancel the unveiling and get everyone to safety. Ol' Jammer warned him that if they waited, the fire would only get worse. André begged Cad to listen to them.

"Who are you? You're a glorified bellboy," Cad said to André. He looked disgustedly at Pulaski. "You're an overpriced sprinkler. And you're"—he stared at Ol' Jammer—"you're old and you've got a dumb hat on!" Cad sounded like a child having a temper tantrum. "Who am I? *I'm* the superintendent, and today is about *me* and *my lodge*!"

He turned back to the crowd to continue with his unveiling. "And now is the moment I've been waiting for!" he said, and dramatically pulled away the tarp to reveal a shiny brass plaque of his own grinning face with the lodge in the background.

Suddenly, a car in the crowd screamed. "Ahhhhh!"

"Now, that's just rude," said Cad, offended.

The screaming car shouted, "Fire!" Everyone turned to see that a nearby mountain was covered in flames! Panic set in as everyone scrambled in multiple directions. It was absolute chaos!

Inside the lodge, André rushed up and down the halls telling everyone to evacuate. Vehicles headed toward the exit and piled onto the train. Ol' Jammer and the secretary of the interior helped usher everyone out.

"This is a mandatory evacuation," said Ol' Jammer calmly.

"Keep moving," said the secretary. "Slowly but surely . . ."

Cad tried to reassure his guests. "No need to panic," he said. "It's just a small fire. At least, come back again. See you next year!"

Outside, Engine Pulaski guided planes on the tarmac. "Remember to avoid the smoke and stay above the canyon walls," he called to the planes as they took off. "All right—next, please."

An old-lady plane rolled up, preparing to take off. She spun her prop, and suddenly—*WHOOSH!* A fancy jet pulled right in front of her.

"Outta my way, taildragger," the jet said rudely.

Pulaski pushed in front of the fancy jet. "Hold on, big fella! No cutsies! You don't wanna upset my buddy here," he said.

Pulaski's assistant, Rake, struck an angry gaze and snapped down his fire shield.

The jet slinked off, terrified.

"All right, ma'am, you're cleared for takeoff," Pulaski said to the old lady.

"Thank you, son," she replied, and flew to safety.

Inside the lodge, once the train was full, it closed its doors. André asked the remaining guests to head to the main road exit. The train whistled as it chugged off, pulling away from the station.

Back at the mine, the fire had finally passed. Blade pushed through the charred debris and slowly rolled out of the mineshaft. He was marked with some bad burns, and one of his tires was melted flat. Dusty coughed as he joined Blade outside the mine. Smoke still filled the air. The burned remains of the forest were blackened and smoking from the heat.

Dusty noticed Blade's burned side. "Blade . . . ," he said, concerned.

But Blade directed Dusty to go to Airway Meadow. He figured they would be clear there to take off. "Let's go," he said, ignoring his injuries.

When they got to the scorched meadow, Dusty revved his engine and rolled across the terrain. It was a little bumpy, but he managed to climb into the air. Blade took off behind him, but before he was more than a few feet off the ground, his engine whined and seized. Blade tilted over and slammed down hard, right into the blackened ground. His rotor tore up chunks of earth until he lay there, completely still.

Dusty circled back and quickly flew down to Blade's side. "BLADE! BLADE!" he called. But Blade didn't answer or even move. Dusty called Patch right away and spoke with urgency: "Blade is down. I repeat, Blade is down."

20

Dipper and Dusty flew alongside Windlifter as he carried Blade to the air attack base. Everyone gathered as Windlifter lowered Blade gently onto the helipad.

"All right! Good! We're good!" shouted Maru. "Pinecone, get these straps off! Avalanche, push the ramp alongside the access panel. And be careful!"

The two smokejumpers quickly got to work. Then Maru rolled up the ramp, opened Blade's panel, and began his examination.

Dusty anxiously turned to Cabbie. "He's going to be okay, right?"

"It's bad, but Maru is the best there is. He'll make him better than new," Cabbie replied.

Maru let out a frustrated sigh. "His hydraulics are fried. He's losing fluids. I got to get him back to the garage, stat." He called Dynamite to get the tow hook.

Dynamite pulled the tow, and Maru hooked Blade up and pulled him to the garage. Maru continued to shout out orders to the others, and everyone worked as a team to help.

"Drip, I'm gonna need hydraulic fluid from the shed."

"You got it!" said Drip.

"Blackout, we'll need another generator. Try the main hangar. And grab another heat lamp."

"I'm on it!" yelled Blackout.

"The surface burns are bad, but the interior damage is repairable," Maru explained. "As long as we move quickly, we've got a good chance. First, we'll stop the leaks, then flush out the debris, and get fresh fluids. After that, I'll need help cleaning out the intakes. They're clogged with smoke and ash. Next, we'll . . ."

Dusty could hear the concern in Maru's voice as his words trailed off. He couldn't believe it. None of this would have happened if he had only listened to Blade. This was all his fault. If Blade didn't make it, Dusty would never forgive himself. He didn't even want to think about that.

Maru worked long hours trying to fix Blade. Later that evening, he finally closed the door to his garage, leaving Blade to rest inside. Dusty timidly rolled up. He wanted to know how Blade was doing, but he was also afraid to ask.

"He's resting now," said Maru. "I've done everything I can."

"Um. Do you think—"

"Look, Dusty, don't blame yourself."

"He should have left me out there," Dusty said sincerely.

"Nah. That ain't Blade's style," Maru said. He paused a moment before continuing. "Especially since . . . what happened to Nick."

"You mean Nick 'Loop'n' Lopez, from the TV show?" Dusty asked.

Maru told Dusty that one day Nick was doing his

trademark loop for a stunt scene when there was an unexpected crosswind. Maru slowly rolled up to the Wall of Fame. He pushed aside a box on his workbench, revealing a picture of Nick "Loop'n" Lopez. "Blade was the first one on the scene. But . . . he didn't know what to do," Maru said.

Dusty couldn't believe it. He could only imagine how horrible Blade must have felt.

"His best friend was gone. And Blade thought his life was over, too." Maru began to busy himself, cleaning up some oil cans while he finished telling the story.

Dusty sadly looked off toward Blade's hangar as he listened.

"But he didn't give up," continued Maru. "He got trained, got certified, and came here. Blade . . . he used to pretend to save lives. Now he saves 'em for real."

Cad watched as the lodge's rooftop sprinklers sprayed weakly. "We're not getting enough water on the lodge!" he yelled at André. "Reroute the main water line to the roof sprinklers."

André refused. "The firefighters need that water to make retardant—"

Cad interrupted him. "How do you know that?"

"I'm the concierge. It's my job to know every—"

"I DON'T CARE!" Cad shouted. "You work for

ME! Now, are you gonna do it, or do I have to do it myself?"

André glared at him in defiance. Seconds later, Cad leaned on the lever with all his might until he finally pushed it into position. With the increased water pressure, the rooftop sprinklers drenched everything in the lodge.

By the exit, a massive traffic jam had formed as hundreds of panicked cars and RVs packed the only route out of the park. Making matters worse was the fact that the exit road was very narrow, with only one lane going in each direction. The raging fire burned on either side of it, and cinders rained down, hissing and popping as they sent sparks all over the road.

Engine Pulaski sprayed water from his nozzle onto the ridge, trying his best to keep the fire from reaching the exit.

Ol' Jammer and the secretary of the interior continued to keep guests quiet and organized. "Don't worry," said Ol' Jammer. "We're gonna get everyone out. Just keep moving and stay calm."

The train appeared, chugging down the tracks toward the exit, when suddenly—*WHOOSH!* A gust of wind blew a wall of flames over the ridge and sent burning debris right in front of the exit tunnel! The train slammed on its brakes, and sparks flew as it came to a screeching stop. With the tunnel blocked, the train was stuck! Cars and RVs gazed up at the fire, terrified.

Then things got even worse. A group of tall pine trees burst into flames, and one of them was lifted right up from its roots as it began to fall over. The giant, flaming pine tumbled down the ridge, bringing an avalanche of fire and rocks with it! Pulaski looked to see Ol' Jammer and the secretary of the interior directly underneath, in the path of the avalanche. "Watch out!" he yelled, pushing them out of the way. *SMASH!* The trees and debris crashed into Engine Pulaski, breaking his nozzle.

The secretary and Ol' Jammer had escaped unharmed, but the nozzle on Pulaski's pump was broken. He could no longer fight the fire.

"We're gonna have to find another way out," the secretary said.

"That's the problem, Mr. Secretary," said Ol' Jammer gravely. "There is no other way out."

Back at the air attack base, the emergency siren blared. "Wildfire jumped the main exit road, and now it's blocked," said Patch over the PA.

"I know it's after sunset, but . . . you're in command," Dipper said, looking to Windlifter. "It's your call."

Windlifter looked up into the sky and then gazed at Dipper.

Maru shouted, "There's not much time. If you're gonna go, you better go now."

"And we'll need every plane we've got," said Dusty.

"Load up," Windlifter said.

Everyone quickly prepared to go out and fight the terrible fire. Maru hooked up the hoses and they puffed to life as they inflated with retardant. The smokejumpers loaded into Cabbie. "We'll have you out of here in sixty sec—"

WHOOSH! Maru was unable to complete his sentence as he heard the loud sound of whooshing air and watched as the hoses sadly deflated. He twisted the valve on the main pipe and squeezed the trigger on the tank's filling hose, but nothing came out. He checked the gauge on the main tank.

"There's no water pressure," Maru said, annoyed.

Without water, he couldn't fill the team's tanks with retardant.

"Main line musta burst again!" Cabbie said.

"Hey, Patch!" shouted Dipper. "What's the lake look like?"

"Negative. No visibility. Boxed in by fire and smoke," Patch replied.

The team looked at each other. What could they do?

"All we have left is what's in our tanks. Let's make it count," said Windlifter. Then he lifted off. Everyone rolled toward the runway and took off, heading toward the main exit road.

As the team soared over the burning landscape, Dusty glanced at his torque gauge. Below, deer tractors stampeded away from the flames as the fire continued to rip through the forest.

"We're headed straight into the fire," Dusty said, concerned. "Aren't we gonna fly around it?"

"The fastest way to the main road is *through* the fire," shouted Dipper.

"Brace yourselves," Windlifter said, and he led them through the smoke. Roaring winds rushed by them as glowing embers and gray ash flew through the air.

The smoke blurred Dusty's vision, and he had trouble seeing where he was going.

Once they flew out of the smoke and made it to the other side, into the valley, they got a good look at the blazing forest. Scattered blackened trees stood among some that were still flaming like gigantic torches. The forest floor was speckled with smoking bare spots and shrubs that were burned to a crisp.

Then they flew past the lodge and noticed the sprinklers dousing the roof. Cad stood nearby, looking up at them as they flew overhead.

Back at the main exit road, Ol' Jammer was still working hard to keep the crowd calm. "Don't panic—everybody'll be all right," he said.

The train, now surrounded by flames, blew his whistle, begging for help. The passengers looked out the window in fear as they watched the flames rise around them.

Finally, the team approached, buzzing above the hopeful cars and RVs below. Windlifter swooped in and dropped his retardant right on target, extinguishing some of the flames. White smoke filled the air as Dipper dropped her retardant . . . right on target. The train blew his whistle again while flames burned both in front and behind it. Dusty glided in and aimed to drop on the fire surrounding the train. He dropped . . . right on target! The cars and RVs on the ground cheered. The fire was out!

"All right," said Dynamite. "Let's clear this road." The smokejumpers landed and cleared the fallen trees and debris, and soon traffic began to move again.

Patch's voice came over the radio. "Windlifter, do you copy?"

"Go ahead, Patch," said Windlifter.

"We've got two old RVs trapped in Augerin Canyon," Patch reported.

Dusty flew up alongside Windlifter. "That's Harvey and Winnie!" he said. "They're looking for where they had their first kiss!"

"Augerin Canyon . . . that's at the other end of the park," said Windlifter.

Dusty had to help them. He told Windlifter he wanted to go. He knew he could get there faster than anyone else.

"The canyon will be engulfed in flames, and you have no retardant," Windlifter said.

"I'll scoop off the river. There's a clear stretch of water."

Windlifter looked at Dusty, considering.

"Windlifter," Dusty pleaded. "I can do it."

"Go," Windlifter said. He watched with concern as Dusty gunned his engine and peeled off, back into the smoke.

22

Dusty tore through the forest as fast as he could, his engine screaming. He looked down at his torque gauge, rising from the green zone into the yellow. He accelerated. He knew he had to get to Winnie and Harvey quickly to have any chance of saving them.

When he reached the two old RVs, they were huddled together in the middle of the burning bridge, terrified. They screamed for help as the flames burned on either side, rapidly getting closer and closer to them. Dusty assessed the situation. He knew he'd have to extinguish one side of the bridge so Winnie and Harvey could drive off safely.

Dusty zoomed down into the canyon, toward the rapids. The fire surrounded him as he flew lower and lower, but he continued. He needed to scoop water into his tank or he wouldn't be able to extinguish the fire. He tried to touch down in the rapids, but a rock outcropping blocked his way. He dodged the rocks and tried again, but it wasn't working.

He steadied himself to gear up for another try, and an army of enormous burning pine trees began to fall right in front of him, as if they were attacking! He rolled left, then right, then left again, avoiding the massive timbers. Two flaming pines fell and spiked down into the ground. Dusty breezed through them as if they were a racing gate.

Dusty was ready to make another attempt at scooping when an avalanche of car-sized boulders tumbled down the hillside. He tried to avoid them, but one of the giant boulders bounced and whacked him on his side. "Aaagh!" he screamed. After several more quick maneuvers, he managed to get past the avalanche to the other side.

Dusty could hear Winnie and Harvey screaming in the distance. He was running out of time and had to act fast. He approached Whitewall Falls and rolled, weaving through the falling trees and rocks that continued to fall all around him.

Over on the burning bridge, Winnie and Harvey cuddled close, fearing for their lives. The bridge was mere seconds from collapsing! They were just about to slip and fall down into the deep canyon when . . . Blade's rotors made a thundering sound as he appeared through the smoke. He lowered his hoist and hooked Harvey, straining to keep the couple from falling off the bridge.

Dusty looked down at the water. He knew it was impossible to make a scoop. But he eyed the falls and had an idea. Determined, he raced toward the falls. His warning light started to flash, and his torque gauge climbed into the red. But Dusty didn't stop. He dove, buzzing beneath the burning bridge, and pulled up sharply. Using every ounce of power, he flew straight into a vertical climb and skimmed the waterfall, scooping water from it!

Then Dusty shot straight up into the air and lost momentum. He hung there for a moment before falling backward, tail first, until his nose dropped back down. Then he torpedoed toward the bridge, skimmed along it, and dropped the water directly onto the fire. Dusty called down to Harvey and Winnie, "The fire's out. Go! Head for the tunnel!"

Blade pulled the hoist, leading Winnie and Harvey back onto the bridge. As the wood splintered and crumbled behind them, Winnie and Harvey raced to safety. Once they got to the tunnel, they shared a kiss.

Dusty flew low over the canyon and saw Harvey and Winnie, safe on the other side of the bridge. He breathed a sigh of relief.

"Dusty—good move, partner," Blade said proudly.

For a brief moment, Dusty felt like he was on top of the world. Then . . . *POP! BANG! GRIIIIIIND-CHUNK!* Dusty's prop made a grinding noise as it came to a sickening halt. His smile vanished as he began to fall from the sky! He smashed through trees, nicking his sides against the thick, protruding branches. Finally, he slammed into the earth. *CRASH!* But Dusty couldn't feel a thing. He was unconscious.

Days later, Dusty woke up inside his hangar feeling groggy and confused. He rolled out into the sunlight and was quickly greeted by the Piston Peak crew.

"He's awake!" shouted Maru when he saw Dusty.

"How long was I out?" Dusty asked.

"Five days," said Blade. "Dipper stayed by your side the whole time."

Dipper leaned in close to Dusty and whispered, "I like watching you sleep."

Cabbie and the smokejumpers rolled up. "HE'S ALIVE!" shouted Avalanche, and the jumpers cheered.

Patch's voice came over the PA. "All aircraft, the superintendent has entered the base."

Ol' Jammer rolled up along with Engine Pulaski and André. Ol' Jammer told Dusty how worried everyone had been about him. They were so happy to see that he was okay.

"You're the superintendent? But what happened to Cad?" Dusty was confused.

Pulaski laughed. "Heh, heh. Sprinklers saved the lodge, but not his job. Secretary of the interior did the right thing and put Ranger Jammer here in charge."

Windlifter turned to Maru. "Did you tell him?"

"I was about to," said Maru.

"Tell me what?" asked Dusty.

"I replaced your prop. Repaired the wing ribs. Hammered out what damage I could. Even got your pontoons back on. But your gearbox . . ."

"Yeah . . . I know," said Dusty, sadly slumping and looking down at the ground. "Thanks for trying, Maru."

"You're welcome!" Maru said excitedly. "Cuz you're fixed!"

"Huh?" Dusty wasn't sure he'd heard him right.

"Wasn't easy. Hardest thing I've ever done. You've got yourself a custom-made epicyclic concentric reduction gearbox!" Maru said proudly.

Dusty was stunned. "A new gearbox?"

"No!" said Maru, offended. "It's *better* than new!"

"Crophopper, I'd say you've earned that certification," said Blade.

Dusty strained and his turbine whined. . . . Then, slowly, his prop spun up and came to full power! He beamed, overjoyed. He couldn't believe it was true—he was fixed! Everyone smiled at Dusty, delighted. They were thrilled to see him back in action. Dusty felt like the luckiest plane in the whole world.

24

Soon after Dusty got back to Propwash Junction, the folks from the TMST returned for an inspection. Ryker and his assistant stood outside the control tower, as they had before. But this time, they brought good news.

"In accordance with CFR title fourteen, volume three, chapter one, section one hundred thirty-nine, subparagraph B, Propwash Junction is recertified and open for business," Ryker said, without a speck of emotion. The notetaking forklift clicked his pen one last time, and everyone in Propwash cheered.

Chug and Sparky rolled up excitedly. "Hey, Dusty! I won, I won! I've been crowned *official* Corn Colonel!" said Chug, proudly wearing a Grand Corn Colonel hat.

"And I'm his Private Niblet!" boasted Sparky.

"Can I wear my official hat to your race next Saturday?" Chug asked Dusty.

"Absolutely," replied Dusty. "As long as the boss here will give me the day off."

"Anytime," said Mayday with a smile.

Chug motioned to Sparky. "Okay, Niblet! Time to hit the festival!"

"Sir, yes, sir! Hey, do you think the deep-fried-corn-cob-on-a-stick guy will be here?" Sparky asked as he followed the Corn Colonel toward the festival.

Mayday rolled over to Dusty. "We're all so proud of you . . . ."

"Thanks, Mayday," Dusty replied.

"What you did for me . . . for all of us . . . I want to thank you," said Mayday.

"You don't have to. . . ."

"Yes, yes, I do," said Mayday. "What you did . . . it takes a special kind of plane."

Dusty was touched.

The gang headed over to the Corn Festival, which was in full swing. The festival was packed, and everyone was having an excellent time. There was corn-themed food, and plenty of fun. Chug got everyone's attention by announcing into the PA, "Ladies and gentleplanes . . . turn your attention to the skies for today's featured aerial presentation. The Propwash Junction Corn Festival is proud to present the Piston Peak Air Attack Team and our very own world-champion racer and certified firefighter . . . Dusty Crophopper!"

The gang from Piston Peak was there! Dusty, Blade, Windlifter, and Dipper roared overhead as the smokejumpers parachuted out of Cabbie. The crowd cheered wildly! The team zoomed over the runway. They performed their routine, doing water drops as the smokejumpers zoomed off several ramps below. Dusty, up in the clouds, dove down sharply, putting on a show for the excited crowd. He released his tank of water, spraying it across the sky. With old friends on the ground and new friends in the sky, Dusty couldn't have felt better. It was great to be a firefighter.